# Mr. Emerson's Cook

✦ Judith Byron Schachner ✦

Dutton Children's Books · New York

*Your work should be in praise of what you love.*
—EMERSON

I must acknowledge with thanks and appreciation, Leslie Wilson of the Concord Free Library Special Collections;
Joann Mente and the guides of the Emerson Home Museum; Donna White Merullo of the Concord Museum; Margaret Compton,
David Emerson, Nancy and Anthony Forbes and their friends the Gates, for inviting us into Lidian's gardens; Sandie Liacouras,
for the Emerson articles; my cousin Robert Byron, for the history; Jolene Borgese, for discovering me; my neighbors Beth and Barbara,
for their support and tears; Kathye Fetsko Petrie, for being an angel on earth. The teachers of Swarthmore-Rutledge School
who over the years have welcomed me into their classrooms; Sara Reynolds, who makes me a better artist;
and my husband, Bob, who has allowed me to pursue my life's work since 1977; and last, my father,
Edward James Byron, for first introducing me to Concord and Emerson. I love you, Dad.

*Library of Congress Cataloging-in-Publication Data*

Schachner, Judith Byron.
Mr. Emerson's cook / by Judith Byron Schachner.—1st ed.
p. cm.
Summary: Annie Burns answers an ad requesting an extraordinary cook
needed to get Mr. Emerson to eat real food to supplement the nourishment
he derives from nature though his imagination.
ISBN 0-525-45884-0 (hc)
I. Emerson, Ralph Waldo, 1803-1882—Juvenile fiction.
[1. Emerson, Ralph Waldo, 1803-1882—Fiction. 2. Food—Fiction.
3. Cookery—Fiction. 4. Imagination—Fiction.] I. Title.
PZ7.S3286Mr 1998 [E]—dc21 98-10032 CIP AC

Published in the United States 1998 by Dutton Children's Books,
a member of Penguin Putnam Inc.
375 Hudson Street, New York, New York 10014
Designed by Ellen M. Lucaire and Sara Reynolds
Printed in Hong Kong
First Edition
1 3 5 7 9 10 8 6 4 2

FOR THE GREAT-GREAT-GRANDDAUGHTERS OF MR. EMERSON'S COOK,

*Emma & Sarah Schachner*

AND FOR

*Lucia Monfried*

WHO TAKES ME BY THE HAND EACH AND EVERY TIME,

WITH LOVE—J.B.S.

The day Annie Burns arrived in the port of Boston from County Fermanagh, Ireland, she set about finding herself a job. Annie scoured the newspapers for work. Positions for maids and scrubwomen were plentiful, but it was a peculiar request that caught her eye. Annie was a good cook, so she decided to apply.

WANTED

*Extraordinary cook needed in the town of Concord, Massachusetts.*
*Acclaimed poet and philosopher has stopped eating due to*
*an overactive imagination and meddlesome Mother Nature.*
*Desperate.*
*Send all inquiries to Mrs. Ralph Waldo Emerson,*
*Cambridge Turnpike, Concord, Massachusetts.*

"There wasn't much food to cook with in my town of Belcoo," Annie wrote to Mrs. Emerson. "But I had a talent for making what little there was taste good."

Annie soon received a reply from Mrs. Emerson and took the next coach to the country town of Concord.

When she arrived at the Emerson home, Annie walked around to the back of the large white house, passing a lovely garden of pinks. She tiptoed around a sleeping dog and shuffled through a small flock of chickens sporting tiny boots on their scratching feet.

"And what manner of humanity might I be cookin' for today?" she asked the chickens.

"The kind which outfits their pets in the finest of footwear."

For a moment Annie thought the chickens or the dog might have spoken to her. Then she looked over her shoulder to see a tall man struggling to lead a calf into the barn.

"Have you come for the cook's job?" asked the man.

"I have indeed, sir," answered Annie, falling into step beside him. "I've crossed an ocean to cook for a man who won't eat—or so the advertisement says."

"Oh, don't trouble yourself over Mr. Emerson," said the man. "Mother Nature provides all he needs."

Annie puzzled over this answer as she walked in front of the calf. Then she stuck her fingers into its mouth and led it easily into the barn.

"I like people who can do things," said the man with a smile.

"Well, I've led many a cow to the barn, but never a philosopher to the dinner table," said Annie as she left him and walked toward the house. "Have yourself a fine day, sir."

Annie straightened her shawl and stood at the open door. Three children chased two kittens around the room while a lady in gray was teaching a parrot to say "pretty."

"Come in," said the lady. "I am Mrs. Emerson."

"And I am Annie Burns, mum."

"Oh, yes, the Irish cook who does so much with so little," said Mrs. Emerson. She looked pleased.

"Papa doesn't eat anymore," shouted the little boy.

"Now, now," said Mrs. Emerson to her son, "it's not that Papa doesn't eat. It's that he doesn't eat enough to suit me.

"My husband is concerned with the feeding of his soul," Mrs. Emerson told Annie, "and I'm concerned with the feeding of all six feet of him."

Annie nodded her head, pretending to understand.

"That's why I advertised for an *extraordinary* cook," said Mrs. Emerson. "It shall take one to win the appetite of such a man."

"Well, mum," Annie said, looking down at her feet, "I think I'm a very good cook who is extraordinarily stubborn. If that'll do, then I'd like the job."

"It will do just fine," said Mrs. Emerson. "Now come with me, girl."

She led Annie into the study, where the gentleman Annie had met earlier by the barn worked at a round table in the middle of the room. In front of him, a book lay open where the ink of newly penned words was drying. "Poems fly from my husband's hand like blackbirds from the trees," said Mrs. Emerson.

"Why, you're Mr. Emerson?" Annie blurted out before she could be properly introduced.

"I am, and if I led you to believe otherwise, I apologize," said Mr. Emerson.

"It's just that I never imagined a famous philosopher doing . . ."

"Work?" suggested Mr. Emerson. "Why, thinking is the hardest task in the world," he added with a chuckle.

A moment later Mrs. Emerson was called away by the children, so Annie stepped closer to the philosopher's desk.

"Is it true you don't eat, sir?" asked Annie.

"Once I had a dream," said Mr. Emerson. "An angel offered me the world in the size and shape of an apple. 'This must thou eat,' said the angel, and I ate the world."

"The last time I ate an apple, sir," said Annie, "'twas merely an apple."

"I admire answers to which no answers can be made," said Mr. Emerson, getting back to his work.

As Annie returned to the kitchen, she remembered hearing about the Riddle of the Great Egyptian Sphinx. "I believe I've just met the Great Sphinx of Concord," she muttered to herself, "and his name is Mr. Emerson."

That evening, Annie wrote a letter home.

*Saints be praised, Mother. I am Mr. Emerson's new cook. He is said to be a famous philosopher and very wise, but to me he seems two cents short of a nickel. What I'll be cooking for this man is a mystery. Angels offer him apples, he says, but will he accept a potato from an Irish Annie? Mrs. Emerson thinks me quite confident, but in the dark corner of my little room, I tremble at the thought of cooking for a man who thinks so much and eats so little.*

*Love, Annie*

The next morning, Annie dressed quickly and rushed down to the kitchen. She made Mr. Emerson's favorite breakfast of pie and hot coffee. Then she carried it to the garden, where the philosopher was watching a brilliant sunrise.

"Are ya doin' some thinking, sir?" asked Annie.

"Why, yes," said Mr. Emerson. "I've been thinking that the sky is the daily bread of the eyes."

Annie looked up and saw nothing resembling a loaf of bread. She placed the tray of food next to the philosopher and walked back to the house, shaking her head. When she came to collect the dishes, the pie and coffee had been left untouched.

So, thought Annie, he prefers the sky to my pie, does he now. And to the dog and chickens, she said, "We'll see about that."

The next day, as Annie hung the dish towels out to dry, she saw Mr. Emerson and his children walking to the woods. He recited the names of every flower and bird they met along the way. And she heard him teaching the children new words in Latin and Greek as he led them to where the lichen grew thick upon the trees. Annie thought them the luckiest children on the earth, to have the world as their classroom and their papa for a teacher.

That evening, Annie placed a large roast wreathed in vegetables at the head of the table. At the other end sat a bowl brimming with buttery potatoes. Mr. Emerson came into the dining room and took his seat. He nibbled on a celery stick and took a bite of a biscuit. Then he pushed his plate away.

"Think me not unkind and rude," he said to his family, "that I walk alone in grove and glen. I go to the God of the wood to fetch his word to men." As he crossed the room, he couldn't help but see the discouraged look on his cook's face, and he said, "The reward of a thing well done is to have done it, Annie."

"Yes, sir, but the reward of a well-cooked meal is to have someone eat it," she declared.

Mr. Emerson just walked out into his yard and gazed up at the stars.

"What angels invented these splendid ornaments?" he asked. But no one had an answer.

Annie was always surprised by Mr. Emerson's unusual way of looking at the world.

"Turn your eyes upside down by looking at the landscape through your legs," he said to her, "and see how agreeable is the picture though you have seen it these twenty years."

"I'll do nothing of the kind," said Annie, laughing out loud at Mr. Emerson's antics. "Things look quite agreeable with my eyes right side up, sir."

Later when she was all alone, Annie scooped up her skirts and did just what Mr. Emerson suggested. She saw an upside-down Bingo, the dog, strolling over to lick her face.

"Och!" said Annie, pushing him away, "I'm as crazy as a philosopher."

Over the months, Annie became devoted to the Emersons. Mr. Emerson had published books of essays and poetry, and he lectured in lyceums around the country, electrifying the crowds of common folk with his thoughts. But for all his brilliance, he did not see the importance of food. And to his cook, this was out of all reason.

When guests descended like bees upon the Emerson home, the buzz of lofty conversation filled the rooms. All manner of ideas were discussed while Annie served tea and cakes to the company. They ate eagerly, but Mr. Emerson did not seem to notice.

"I like that every chair should be a throne and hold a king," said Mr. Emerson to his circle of friends. How comfortable he seemed among the poets, politicians, and philosophers who visited. Yet Annie knew he cherished his conversations with the chickadees just as much.

Annie wrote to her mother of all the goings-on at the Emersons', and of her troubles.

*Lord knows I try to understand Mr. Emerson, but his wisdom escapes me. When offered a warm bowl of soup, he chooses the warm colors of the sunset every time. He told me, "There is wonder enough in my thumbnail already." My wonder is why I bite mine. I do admire his ability to find happiness in simple pleasures, but then why won't he eat what I make? Mrs. Emerson has not released me from service—yet, though I have sorely failed in my task. So, please, Mother, if you have good advice, send it soon. I wish only to succeed as Mr. Emerson's cook.*

*Love, Annie*

Winter brought snow to the roads and rooftops of Concord. Mr. Emerson found monsters and white rabbits in the boughs of the balsam firs. He saw a mastodon in the mighty elms. But no matter how hard Annie tried to see these things, she could not.

"We live by our imaginations" was one of Mr. Emerson's sayings. But Annie did not understand these words. She felt as if her own imagination was frozen solid without the hope of a summer day to melt it.

The next day, Annie received a package. She tore the wrapper away from a ragged little book with a note attached. It read:

> Dearest Annie,
> It pains me to think of you having problems with Mr. Emerson's appetite. He sounds like a decent man who should warm to your fine cooking in due time.
> I was cleaning behind the cupboard this morning when I came upon the cook-book you made as a wee child. Remember the recipes for mud pies and moon cakes, Annie? They are all there just as you wrote them. I don't know how, but it might help with your predicament.
> Be a good girl, and say your prayers.
>
> Mother

Annie couldn't imagine what her mother was thinking of, so she put the book aside until bedtime.

That night, a chilly wind rattled the windows of Annie's room. She shivered as she crawled beneath her quilts and began to read by the light of the icy moon:

"A cup full of clouds, three spoons of gray sky, the song of a lark, one stone smooth and dry."

Though it was the coldest of nights, Annie grew warm. The more she read, the hotter she became, until Annie felt as if the sun itself bore down upon her head. She threw off her quilts and opened the window. As she drew in a cold breath, Annie remembered another of Mr. Emerson's sayings: "Imagination is to flow, not to freeze."

At that moment Annie understood what he was saying. She looked up and saw the stars truly for the first time. She held her little book next to her heart and let her imagination flow....

Annie imagined setting a glittering table. The sun was poured into heavenly cups, and silverware sparkled by the light of the moon. A comet-tail stew she prepared was so spicy-hot, it sent guests into orbit around the room. The planets applauded Mr. Emerson's cook while the philosopher ate from everyone's plate.

Annie imagined serving a snow pudding that shimmered beneath a cloud of vanilla custard. Four little women sat side by side at Mr. Emerson's table.

"Delightful," said the one named Louisa.

The more they ate, the colder it grew. Frost etched patterns on their crystal goblets, and snow began to fall from the ceiling. All the while summer hummed like a bee outside the window.

Annie imagined a broccoli forest alight with yellow melting butterflies as she looked out the window toward the woods. Beside it was a steaming pond of soup. The sight was so beautiful that Mr. Emerson's friend Henry Thoreau built a cabin by the pond right in the middle of dinner.

That night, Annie slept warmly by the open window. Her imagination continued to flow right into her delicious dreams.

The next morning, Annie woke before dawn. She smoothed her starched white apron over her dress and carried her little book down into the kitchen. "If we are to live by our imagination," she said, "then we must cook with it."

Annie opened the book to her recipe for Sunrise Pie. She placed a large bowl beside an open window and watched as it filled with all the colors of the morning sky. The wind blew in birdsong and sunbeams, while the earth lent its sweetness to the golden apples and cinnamon spice Annie added. She poured the confection into a tender crust and tucked the pie into a hot oven.

Before long, Mr. Emerson appeared in the kitchen.

"What heavenly ambrosia wakes me from my sleep?" he asked.

"Good morning to you, sir," said Annie, "and have yourself a wee taste of the morning sun."

With Mr. Emerson's first bite, a dazzling light filled his head.

"I am the sun!" he said, and climbed on top of his chair. "I expand and live in the warm day like corn and melon," he cried.

Annie cried, too, but they were tears of joy, for she had succeeded in winning back Mr. Emerson's appetite.

Mrs. Emerson came into the kitchen, but she couldn't believe the sight of her husband eating Annie's pie. The children squealed and scrambled around their father's legs, shouting, "We want to be the sun, too."

So Annie fed them all her glorious pie and watched as their faces smiled brighter than the sun in the sky.

As the family enjoyed their breakfast together, Annie stepped outside. Snowflakes began to fall, and her skirts lifted as she twirled in the wind. Annie felt full of happiness.

After two more helpings of Annie's pie, Mr. Emerson retired to his study, where he spent the day writing. Before dinner he found Annie peeling potatoes at the kitchen sink. He handed her a piece of paper and walked back into his room. Annie dried her hands on her apron and carefully unfolded the note. Then she read Mr. Emerson's words.

*What lies behind us*
*and what lies before us*
*are small matters compared*
*to what lies within us.*

*A friend may well be reckoned*
*the masterpiece of nature.*

Annie smiled as she tucked the note into her apron pocket. She carried the potatoes over to the pot on the stove and tossed them into her fish chowder. A fog lifted from the pot and floated all the way down the hall into Mr. Emerson's study. He heard seagulls cry and tasted the salty air upon his lips, and he knew it was time for his dinner.

# Afterword

Ralph Waldo Emerson was born in Boston, Massachusetts, on May 25, 1803. He attended Boston Latin School and at the age of fourteen entered Harvard College. Around the age of nineteen, Emerson began keeping a journal. He liked to call it his "savings bank," and for over fifty years he regularly deposited into it a wealth of thoughts, observations, and ideas. This careful examination of his life and times, a remarkable "march of Mind," helped Emerson develop into one of America's greatest thinkers. He was, for a brief time, a Unitarian minister, but after the death of his beloved wife, Ellen, he took a different path. He resigned from the Second Church of Boston and sailed for Europe. Emerson took this time not just to visit countries but to travel the landscape of his "inner soul." This became his lifelong journey.

In 1835 Emerson remarried and brought his new wife, Lidian, to the New England town of Concord, Mass. It was in this lovely rural setting that Emerson was inspired to write so stirringly about Man and his relationship to God and Nature. Influenced by the Romantics, the philosophy of Transcendentalism he espoused included a belief in man's divinity and unity with Nature, and an emphasis on individualism, self-reliance, and following one's own intuition rather than an outside authority.

When Emerson was thirty-four, he met fellow Concord resident Henry David Thoreau. This kindred spirit, many years younger than Emerson, enjoyed long walks as much as Emerson did. Thoreau stayed with the Emersons often, exchanging room and board for gardening and carpentry. Emerson admired Thoreau's self-sufficiency, independence, and ability to "do things." Thoreau's rebellious nature amused his older friend: "Everything that boy does makes merry with society," Emerson noted in his journal. While Thoreau did all he could to avoid leading a conventional life, Emerson lived well within the constraints of society.

The Emerson children adored "their Mr. Thoreau." He would pop corn for them using an old bed warmer and pretend to swallow a book whole, much to the amazement of his giggling audience. Lidian referred to these times as "Henry's second childhood." The eccentric Thoreau with his haunting blue eyes, whose own writing would later inspire Mahatma Gandhi and the Reverend Martin Luther King, Jr., was the same man who sewed tiny buckskin boots for Lidian's chickens. It has been said that they kept the birds from scratching up Lidian's flower beds and warmed their scrawny little feet in winter.

Both men were fierce opponents of slavery. In the years before the Civil War, Emerson confessed, "I do not wish to live in a nation where slavery exists." He and Lidian offered their home as a haven for fugitive slaves. He praised Great Britain for abolishing the institution, proclaiming the event a "day of reason, of clear light." He and Thoreau spoke and wrote against the government and advocated following one's own conscience rather than the laws of an unjust state. He wanted the nation to begin anew: "What answer is it now to say it has always been so."

My own introduction to Mr. Emerson occurred when I was a child. My father, the grandson of Annie Burns Byron, would bring me to the town of Concord to swim in Walden Pond and stand in the place where the embattled farmers, in Emerson's words, "fired the shot heard round the world." We visited Mr. Emerson's house, and I would beg my father to tell me again the story about my great-grandmother, who was Mr. Emerson's cook.

Ann Burns and her sister Rose worked as domestics for the Emersons. Annie eventually married James Byron, and together they had eleven children. They lived happily in Concord for the rest of their lives. My great-grandfather was keeper of the Old North Bridge. But that's another story. . . .

*Judith Byron Schachner*